The Parrot Tico Tango

Written and illustrated by ANNA WITTE

Sung by BRIAN AMADOR

Barefoot Books
Step inside a story

The parrot Tico Tango
Had a round, **yellow** mango,

But it wasn't quite as yellow
As the lemon of Marcello.

And Tico Tango knew
That he had to have it too,
So he took it!

The parrot Tico Tango
Had a round, yellow mango,

And he carried to his right
A lemon small and bright,

When he spied Elena's fig,
Which was **purple**, sweet and big.

And Tico Tango knew
That he had to have it too,
So he grabbed it!

The parrot Tico Tango
Had a round, yellow mango,

And he carried to his right
A lemon small and bright,

And on his left, a fig,
Which was purple, sweet and big,

When he noticed his friend Terry
With a **red**, juicy cherry.

And Tico Tango knew
That he had to have it too,
So he stole it!

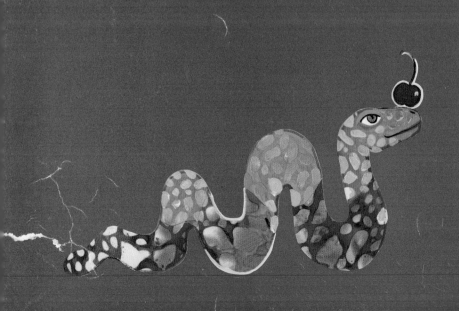

The parrot Tico Tango
Had a round, yellow mango,

And he carried to his right
A lemon small and bright,

And on his left, a fig,
Which was purple, sweet and big,

And on his back, from Terry,
A red, juicy cherry,

When he saw Marina munch
On a **green** grape bunch.

And Tico Tango knew
That he had to have it too,
So he snatched it!

The parrot Tico Tango
Had a round, yellow mango,

And he carried to his right
A lemon small and bright,

And on his left, a fig,
Which was purple, sweet and big,

And on his back, from Terry,
A red, juicy cherry,

And he clutched the grapes he'd put
In his strong sharp foot,

When he spotted proud Soraya
With a deep **orange** papaya.

And Tico Tango knew
That he had to have it too,
So he seized it!

The parrot Tico Tango
Had a round, yellow mango,

And he carried to his right
A lemon small and bright,

And on his left, a fig,
Which was purple, sweet and big,

And on his back, from Terry,
A red, juicy cherry,

And he clutched the grapes he'd put
In his strong sharp foot,

And in his other foot he held
The papaya he had smelled,

When he saw his good friend Nate
With a tiny, **brown** date.

And Tico Tango knew
That he had to have it too!

So he opened his beak wide

To fit it deep inside, when ...

Now, the parrot Tico Tango
Didn't even have his mango!

But his friends thought: what a treat!
All that fruit they had to eat!

They took the fruit he stole
And they put it in a bowl,

They washed it and they sliced it,
They peeled it and they diced it.

Tico Tango felt contrite.
He knew he had to put things right.

'Please forgive me, I feel bad
That I took the fruit you had.'

And the parrot Tico Tango
Begged for just one piece of mango.

His friends were quite divided,
But soon they all decided

He deserved another chance:
They would make the parrot dance!

'If you teach us all to tango
You can have a piece of mango!'

And Tico Tango knew
That he had to have it too,

So he danced for it!

For Alex,

with whom I ran barefoot along a beach in southern Costa Rica,

where we first saw Tico Tango — A. W.

Barefoot Books
294 Banbury Road
Oxford, OX2 7ED

Barefoot Books
2067 Massachusetts Ave
Cambridge, MA 02140

Text and illustrations © 2004 by Anna Witte
The moral rights of Anna Witte have been asserted
Lead vocals, guitar and programming © 2011 by Brian Amador
Additional vocals by Rosi and Alisa Amador; saxophones played by Tim Mayer
Recorded and produced by Amador Bilingual Voiceovers, Cambridge, MA, USA

First published in Great Britain by Barefoot Books, Ltd
and in the United States of America by Barefoot Books, Inc in 2004
This paperback edition first published in 2011
All rights reserved

Graphic design by Barefoot Books, Bath
Reproduction by Grafiscan, Verona
Printed in China on 100% acid-free paper by Printplus, Ltd
This book was typeset in Toddler and Sassoon Primary
The illustrations were prepared in fabrics, acrylic pen, paper, ink and pastels

ISBN 978-1-84686-669-2

British Cataloguing-in-Publication Data:
a catalogue record for this book is available from the British Library

Library of Congress Cataloging-in-Publication Data is available under
LCCN 2004020040

5 7 9 8 6